AYMAN'S IFTAR

Written by Stephanie Boyle
Illustrated by Kevin Soeria Jaya

As soon as the alarm rang in the darkness, Ayman sat up on his bed and rubbed the sleep from his big brown eyes. He tiptoed softly down the stairs thinking about the day ahead. Being ten years old this was Ayman's third year of fasting in Ramadan and like everything else he put his mind to, Ayman took fasting seriously. Downstairs in the kitchen, Mum and Baba were quietly preparing a lot of food and drink and placing them on the table for *Suhoor*, the pre-dawn meal.

There were biscuits and a pot of hot coffee for Baba, fresh fruits and tea for Mum and, best of all, there was a big pan on the stove with mounds of golden batter bubbling and turning into pancakes. Ayman knew that in a few short minutes those pancakes would be sitting in a stack on his favourite plate, piping hot and dripping with delicious amber syrup, all for him.

He loved this time of day when the house was still and peaceful. Mummy moved with clockwork precision around the kitchen, his little brother and sister were still in bed and he had time to anticipate the day ahead. Ayman looked up to thank his mother for making his favourite pre-fasting treat. She looked exhausted. It was the 20th day of Ramadan. Their home had been filled with joy and a celebratory atmosphere all month long and he knew that she was responsible for it. She had been decorating, cooking, cleaning, crafting and entertaining in addition to worshipping all month.

In that instant, he knew exactly what he wanted to do. "Mum?" Ayman said. "Would you take me to the supermarket today? I want to try and cook *Iftar* for everyone tonight!" His mother looked down at him with a tired smile. "Oh, darling, that's such a beautiful idea but I'm really not sure. Making food for *Iftar* is a big job even for adults, bigger than you can imagine. It's also a really big responsibility making sure that the food is ready for everyone on time."

Ayman's face fell.

He genuinely wanted to help his mother. His disappointment did not go unnoticed, so his mother added, "But if you're sure this is something you really want to do, then I'd love to give you a chance. But let me tell you, just the fact that you wanted to do this makes me so grateful. *Ma sha Allah*, you're really growing up and becoming the incredible, thoughtful young man I made *dua* for!"

With a tummy full of his mother's pancakes and enough water to ensure he wouldn't get dehydrated during the day, Ayman prayed *Fajr* and then snuggled back under the quilt in his cosy bed. Before he knew it, the sun was shining through the window, and he could hear birds chirping outside. He rubbed the sleep from his eyes and prepared to get up for the second time that day when his little brother Younes landed with a loud thump on his bed. "Hey, Ayman! It's nice and sunny outside and Baba said we can go to the park! Let's have a ride and race our scooters. Or we can try to get to the top of that big tree!"

Ayman was about to say yes to the park when he realised that he had a whole day of cooking ahead of him. "Nope. Sorry. I can't. I told Mum I'd be making *Iftar* today and that's a huge responsibility!" he told his brother, echoing his mother's words. Younes continued to bounce on the bed and then transformed into a Spinosaurus (his current favourite dinosaur), determined to devour his brother, but Ayman quickly sprang out of bed, avoiding Younes's imaginary claws and sharp teeth.

He made his way downstairs and went straight to the bookshelf where his mother kept the recipe books. He had decided to make a soup, a salad, some type of meat dish and then a truly scrumptious cake for dessert but he still needed to look up some recipes for inspiration and most importantly, he had to make a list of ingredients. A bright blue and orange coloured book spine caught his eye.

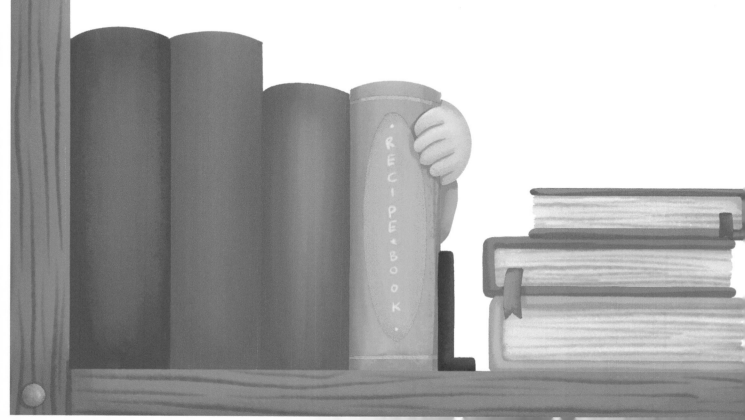

Ayman pulled it from the shelf and sat down with it on his lap. It was a collection of recipes inspired by the Maghreb - a group of countries in North Africa including Algeria where his Baba was from. Looking through the book, Ayman could almost smell and taste the photographs and recipes in it, fighting back the first pangs of hunger.

In no time, Ayman had his menu. He decided on harira soup, meatball tagine and an orange and almond cake. Taking a pen and paper from the table, he diligently began writing down his list of ingredients. However, just as he reached the last couple of ingredients, his little sister Maisara barrelled into the room shrieking with a mixture of fear and joy as Younes the Spinosaurus chased after her. Ayman snatched up his paper and the cookbook just in time before the two of them crashed right where he had been seated a few seconds ago. "Hey! Watch out!" he shouted, but they were already long gone.

An hour later, Ayman and his mother arrived at the supermarket. His mother reached for the shopping trolley, but Ayman stopped her, smiling. "Let me do it. I'm in charge today!" his mother laughed and let him choose a trolley. Ayman led the way confidently through the fresh produce, the deli, the bakery and up and down the many aisles, choosing everything he needed to make his dishes and ticking each item off as it was added to the trolley. With just a couple of ingredients remaining, he turned the corner into the next aisle and narrowly missed crashing into his friend Matheen.

While Ayman and Matheen talked about school, Ramadan, potential Eid presents, sports and their current favourite movies, their mothers also caught up. All of a sudden, Ayman's mum looked down at her watch and was shocked to see how much time had passed.

"Oh wow! Ayman, we need to get going if you're going to finish cooking before *Maghrib*." They bid Matheen and his mum *Salam* and raced to the cash registers … completely forgetting the final two items on the list.

When they arrived home, Ayman leapt out of his seat and started up the stairs. His mother called out to remind him to come and help her with the bags. "Sorry," Ayman said sheepishly. He'd simply been too excited to start cooking.

Ayman scooped up an armful of bags from the boot of the car, but in his haste, one of the bags slipped from his grasp and fell with a crash to the ground. He squatted down and collected everything … except for two oranges that had rolled across the ground and settled right underneath the car, out of reach and out of sight.

Finally in the kitchen and ready to start work, it immediately became apparent to Ayman that things weren't exactly going to plan. For starters, after he had softened the onion and added the spices to the enormous silver pot for the soup, he couldn't find the vegetable stock and realised that despite it being in the list of ingredients, it wasn't on his shopping list.

Oh well, thought Ayman. Surely stock was just flavoured water, right? Once the soup was made, with its spices, vegetables and lentils, the water he added would be extremely flavoursome, he thought.

As Ayman prepared to move on to his next dish, Younes bounded into the kitchen, his favourite T-rex swinging wildly. He spied the bag of red lentils on the countertop and before Ayman could say a word, plunged the dinosaur headfirst into it, lentils flying everywhere. "Roar!!! It's a volcanic explosion!" Younes cried, and was off again, stomping out through the front door to the garden and beyond.

RAWRR!

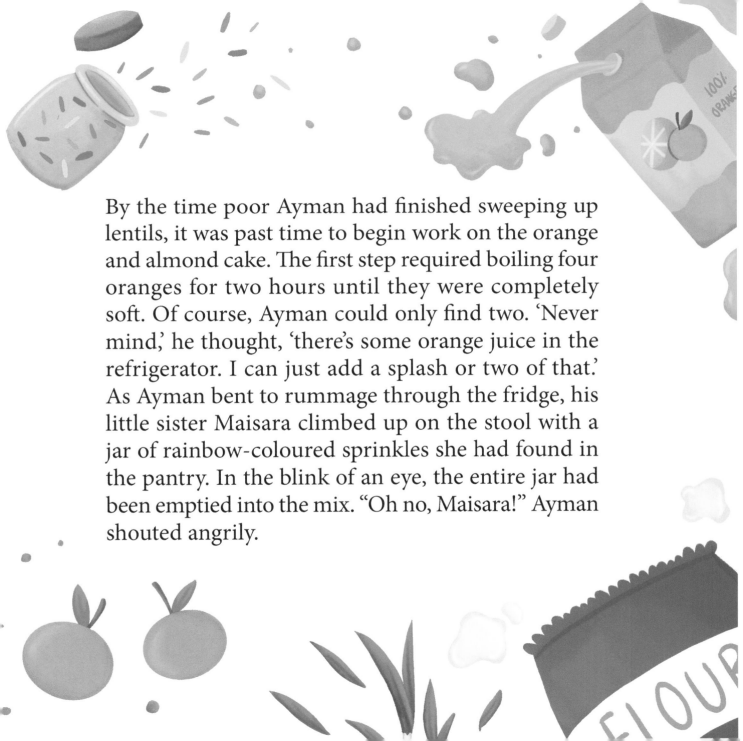

By the time poor Ayman had finished sweeping up lentils, it was past time to begin work on the orange and almond cake. The first step required boiling four oranges for two hours until they were completely soft. Of course, Ayman could only find two. 'Never mind,' he thought, 'there's some orange juice in the refrigerator. I can just add a splash or two of that.' As Ayman bent to rummage through the fridge, his little sister Maisara climbed up on the stool with a jar of rainbow-coloured sprinkles she had found in the pantry. In the blink of an eye, the entire jar had been emptied into the mix. "Oh no, Maisara!" Ayman shouted angrily.

As his frustration built, he remembered his fast and took a deep breath. He shook his head at her as she ran away giggling, her curls bouncing. Peering into the mixing bowl Ayman surveyed the damage. 'It's okay' he decided, 'maybe a bit more fun with rainbow sprinkles than without.'

Ayman's last task was to get to work on the meatball tagine. He chopped and sautéed onions, added the diced tomato and began to look for the special *Ras-el-hanout* spice mix. It was missing too! 'No worries,' thought Ayman, 'all the best chefs are experimental.'

As he added a range of other spices he found in the pantry to the sauce, he imagined that he was creating a new taste sensation, the likes of which had never been created before. He imagined writing his own recipes and being a celebrated gastronome, the youngest culinary superstar in the world!

As everything bubbled and baked away in the kitchen, Ayman called his brother and sister. Together, they rummaged through his mother's linen collection to select their favourite tablecloth and napkins. They set the table for what was certain to be a memorable evening. Before long, the table looked like a little piece of North Africa in the Australian suburbs.

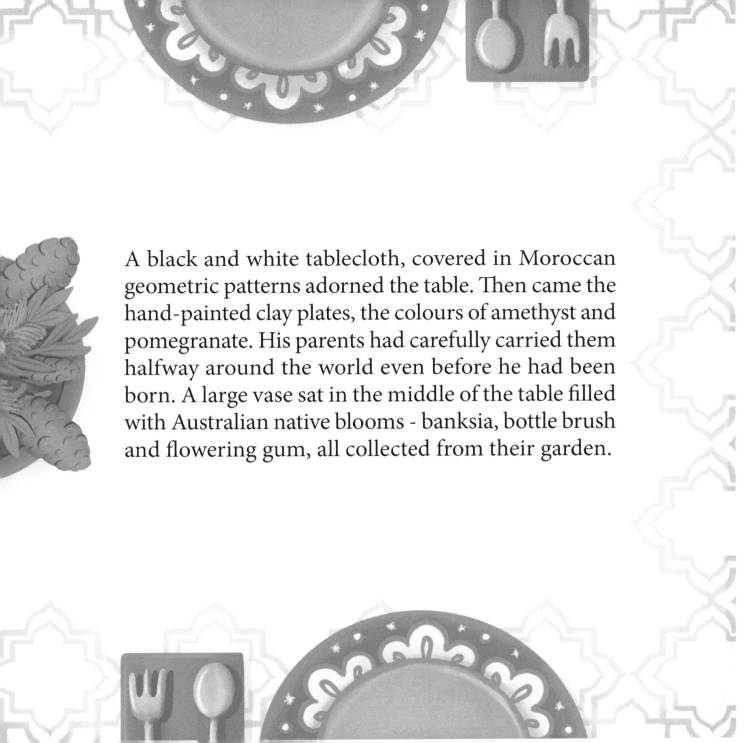

A black and white tablecloth, covered in Moroccan geometric patterns adorned the table. Then came the hand-painted clay plates, the colours of amethyst and pomegranate. His parents had carefully carried them halfway around the world even before he had been born. A large vase sat in the middle of the table filled with Australian native blooms - banksia, bottle brush and flowering gum, all collected from their garden.

Before he knew it, the sky outside the kitchen window was darkening to a shade of purple and the sun was offering up its last rays of light for the day. Ayman knew that *Maghrib* was just minutes away. His mother, who had been keeping a watchful eye from a distance all afternoon, came into the kitchen to assist him. She hugged him and planted a heartfelt kiss on his forehead. "Ayman," she said, "I want you to know that no matter how everything turns out this evening, I am enormously proud of your efforts, the thought you put into preparing *Iftar* for everyone and your desire to help me. And you've managed to do all of this while fasting! May Allah reward you abundantly in this life and the next."

The family gathered at the beautifully set table to enjoy all of Ayman's hard work. As they took their first sips of water and tasted the sweet dates, they made *dua*. Ayman looked around the table excitedly, anticipating his family's joy when they tried his amazing food. But instead, to his surprise and horror, he saw his father's raised eyebrows, his brother's grimace and his sister pushing her bowl as far away from her as possible. Ayman knew at that moment that his *Iftar* had been a total disaster. He pushed his chair back with a screech and ran upstairs, heartbroken.

A few moments later, his mother joined him, and perched on the edge of the bed. As she smoothed the hair on his forehead and wiped his tears, she spoke to him in a soothing voice. "Ayman, cooking is a science and an art that takes years of practice. That being said, I know loads of adults who couldn't have achieved what you did today, and you did it with so much love! You will learn from what went wrong and next time, everything will be much smoother *in sha Allah*."

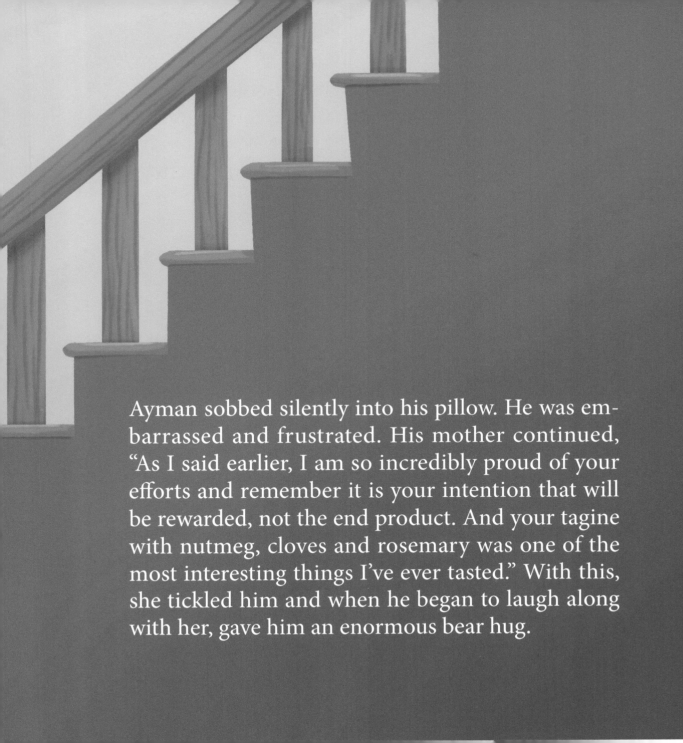

Ayman sobbed silently into his pillow. He was embarrassed and frustrated. His mother continued, "As I said earlier, I am so incredibly proud of your efforts and remember it is your intention that will be rewarded, not the end product. And your tagine with nutmeg, cloves and rosemary was one of the most interesting things I've ever tasted." With this, she tickled him and when he began to laugh along with her, gave him an enormous bear hug.

"Also," Ayman's mother went on, "despite the big deal we make of it and the effort we put into it, *Iftar* isn't the most important part of fasting. We know from our Prophet Mohammed that the breaking of the fast is a moment of joy, but it's not because of the quality or quantity of food that we break it with."

"I just wanted it to be perfect," Ayman said, eyes downcast. "If the food doesn't make everyone happy then what does?"

"Well," continued his mother, "People breaking their fast feel happy knowing that they have obeyed Allah and controlled themselves in order to make Him happy. You should also know that those who fast have a special reward waiting for them when they meet Allah. So, while a delicious *Iftar* is awesome right now, the true reward comes later, even if all we ever manage to break our fast with is a stale piece of bread ... or a slightly unusual orange cake with rainbow sprinkles!" His mother's words were a balm to Ayman. He sat up and snuggled into her. "So, let's go downstairs, Baba has a surprise for you."

Baba, Younes and Maisara weren't at the table anymore when Ayman and his mum arrived downstairs. They were waiting in the car. "Where are we going?" Ayman asked in surprise. "You'll see soon!" his mother answered.

The car wove through the now darkened city suburbs. Soon Ayman knew exactly where they were and when they hopped out of the car in the suburb of Lakemba, he was filled with excitement. Lakemba was home to the famous Ramadan Night Market, an entire street filled with stalls selling amazing food and drink.

There were juicy camel burgers on the grill, golden, buttery corn on the cob, steaming, creamy *sahlep* sprinkled with fragrant nutmeg and cinnamon, golden *zalabia* and spicy curries of all descriptions. Bright decorative lamps lit up the deep night sky. Shop windows were filled with sparkling crescent moons and signs wishing everyone 'Ramadan Mubarak'. Men in *fez* and gold embroidered velvet vests called out to the people, laughing and gesturing to their wares.

Ramadan Mubarak

A man on a beautiful Arabian horse cantered up and down the middle of the street, and children carried swirling wands of flashing lights. The entire street was a feast for the senses as fragrances, sounds and sights wafted around them. As he munched on a corn on the cob, Ayman felt an enormous sense of relief and joy about how the day had come to an end and also, that the most important part of his day, his fast, had been a success.

Ayman's Iftar, 2023

Graphic Design: Teresa Saldaña
Editing: Samira Issa

©Uhibbook Publishing

ISBN: 9789948796732

www.uhibbook.com

Approved by National Media Council U.A.E